Dedicated to

My Grandmother Nell, who helped me understand that they
were not just names on dusty old records, but all real people.

NHJ

and to Annie, who taught me to care.

BHL

Published in 2003 by Simply Read Books Inc.

Cataloguing in Publication Data

Jorgensen, Norman, 1954-
In Flanders Fields/ Norman Jorgensen; Brian Harrison-Lever, illustrator

Includes bibliographical references.
ISBN 1-8949965-01-9

1. World War, 1914-1918 - Juvenile fiction. I. Title.
PZ7.J77In2003   j823   C2003-910262-9

First published by Fremantle Arts Centre Press
Consulting Editor Ray Coffey
Production Coordinator Cate Sutherland
Designed by Marion Duke

Printed and bound in Singapore

Simply Read Books Inc.
501-5525 West Boulevard
Vancouver, B.C. V6M 3W6
www.simplyreadbooks.com

IN FLANDERS FIELDS

NORMAN JORGENSEN
& BRIAN HARRISON-LEVER

Simply Read Books

Early on Christmas morning the guns stop firing. A deathly silence creeps over the pitted and ruined landscape.

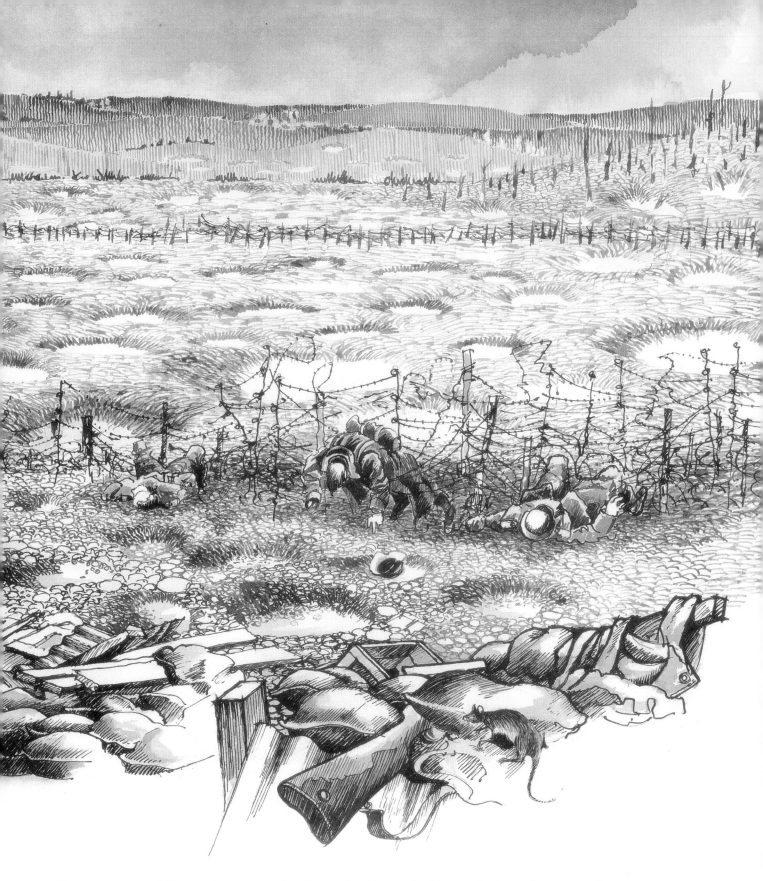

For many soldiers the sound of exploding shells and the chatter of machine-guns continues in their heads; their minds damaged by the weeks of deafening noise.

Men step down from the raised firing boards into the slush of the trench and drink strong scalding tea. Their tin cups shake uncontrollably in the cold morning air.

Mail has been delivered and is handed out. Sadly, many letters and parcels have to be returned to the mail sack.

But one young soldier remains peering through a periscope over the top of the trench. Way out in no-man's-land, he sees a small red shape moving on the barbed wire.

A brightly coloured robin is trapped. One wing is flapping helplessly.
The bird is unable to free itself from the tangle of deadly barbs.

Reluctantly, the young soldier turns away. He walks down the trench to get his mail and warm himself by the small fire.

From home they have sent him a Christmas card and a white silk scarf. A letter brings news of his family, school friends and neighbours in a world that seems years away.

Eventually, the young soldier leaves the warmth of the fire and returns to his place on the firing line. The robin is still trapped. He imagines he can hear it screeching in pain and fear.

Taking the silk scarf from its Christmas wrapping, he ties it to the bayonet on the end of his rifle. Slowly he raises it as a white flag of truce above the top of the trench.

No shots ring out. He lifts his helmet up.
Still no shots. Slowly and carefully he crawls up the ladder
until his head and shoulders are showing. Cautiously, step by step he begins
to walk out into no-man's-land.

From his shell hole a sniper lines the cross on his sights with the middle of the soldier's chest. He takes the slack from the trigger, but waits.

The young soldier walks on, the white silk scarf hanging limply from the bayonet.

Another sniper brings his sights onto the young man's
face. The eyes and nose are red from the cold and the lingering gas of
a recent attack.

A machine-gunner pulls back the bolt on the side of his gun. But still the
young soldier walks slowly forward, his boots crunching in the iced black
mud of the frozen battlefield.

Finally, he reaches the wire. He puts down his rifle,
and gently frees the bird.

Raising the bird above his head, he lets it go.

It flies towards the enemy lines, but crashes to the ground after a few metres, its wings beating feebly.

The soldier walks forward and gently picks up the bird. He stands holding it tenderly in both hands, warming it against the chill.

He is a solitary figure in the huge, desolate battle ground.
More rifles are aimed at him.

After a long time he again lifts the bird and lets it go. This time it flies up and away.

He whispers softly, 'Merry Christmas, little bird.'

A sniper whispers to himself, '*Gluckliche Weihnacht*, Digger!'
and lowers his rifle.

The young soldier turns back to his own lines and, forgetting his rifle and scarf, walks towards his trench.

And as he walks away, from the trenches behind him he can hear hoarse, lonely voices beginning to sing:

Stille nacht, heilige nacht ...

Then, as he gets closer to his own trench, he hears the carol continue:

all is calm, all is bright
Round yon Virgin Mother and Child
Holy Infant so tender and mild
Sleep in heavenly peace
Sleep ...

In Flanders fields the poppies blow
Between the crosses, row on row,
That mark our place; and in the sky
The larks, still bravely singing, fly
Scarce heard amid the guns below.

(*from* 'In Flanders Fields', John McCrae, 1872–1918)